Happy Cat First Readers

The Gorilla Suit

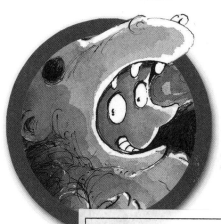

Victor Kelleher

Illustrated by
Stephen Michael King

Published by
Happy Cat Books
An imprint of Catnip Publishing Ltd
Islington Business Centre
3-5 Islington High Street
London N1 9LQ

First published by Penguin Books, Australia, 2002

This edition first published 2006
1 3 5 7 9 10 8 6 4 2

Text copyright © Victor Kelleher, 2002
Illustrations copyright © Stephen Michael King, 2002

A CIP catalogue record for this book is available
from the British Library

ISBN 10: 1 905117 26 4
ISBN 13: 978-1-905117-26-0

Printed in Poland

www.catnippublishing.co.uk

Happy Cat First Readers

The Gorilla Suit

Tom loved the gorilla
suit he was given for
his birthday. He wears
it everywhere, even to
the zoo. Then he gets
to meet the real
gorillas and things get
very complicated
indeed.

For Walter, Caspar,

Charlie and Cecily. *V.K.*

For the Cowan Kids. *S.M.K.*

Chapter One

Tom was given a gorilla suit for his birthday.
He loved it. He wore it everywhere. He even wore it the day Mum and Dad took him to the zoo.

'You'll bake in that,' Dad said.

1

'Waugh!' Tom answered in his gruffest voice. He sounded just like a gorilla.

'Why not wear ordinary clothes for once?' Mum pleaded.

'Waugh!' Tom said again, and beat both hands on his chest.

So Mum and Dad gave in and took him as he was.

When they reached the zoo, Tom went looking for

gorillas. He climbed on a

wall, and there they were.

A whole family of them.

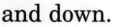

He felt really excited.

He started jumping up

and down.

'Waugh!' he shouted.

'Waugh-waugh-waugh!'
the gorillas answered.

Tom jumped higher still.

'Careful!' Dad said. But

the warning came too late.

Tom had already
slipped. He fell into the
gorilla pen.

Luckily, a female gorilla
was sitting below the wall.
He landed right in the
middle of her soft furry belly.

'Waugh!' she grunted,
and gave Tom a lick. Then
a cuddle. Then tucked him
under her arm.

'My baby boy!' Mum
shrieked.

'Somebody fetch the keeper!' Dad shouted.

The keeper arrived a few minutes later, with a net

on a long pole. He looked
down into the pen. He
couldn't see a boy anywhere.
Just two baby gorillas

romping together on the
grass.

'One of those is our Tom,'
Dad told him.

'The handsome one,' Mum
said.

They looked about the same to the keeper. He reached down with the net and scooped one up.

'Waugh!' said the youngster.

Mum made a grab for him. 'That's Tom all right. I'd know his gorilla voice anywhere.'

She and Dad took him off home.

Chapter Two

That night at dinner, Tom
wouldn't take off his gorilla
suit. He wouldn't use his
knife and fork. He wouldn't
eat his meat either.

He was only interested
in the vegetables. In his
pumpkin, cabbage and peas.

12

He crammed them into his
mouth with both hands.
Then licked the furry
fingers of his gorilla suit.

'I don't know what's got
into him,' Mum complained.

'He usually hates pumpkin.'
Tom crawled across the
table and helped himself
to his dad's pumpkin.

'Well, he seems to like it now,' Dad said.

Tom ate Dad's peas too. He really enjoyed those.

'Waugh!' he said, and sat down in Dad's plate.

Next, he hopped across to the fruit-dish on the sideboard.

'Goodness me!' Dad said. 'I've never seen a banana go down as quick as that before.'

The second banana went
down even quicker. So did
two ripe pears, a bunch of
grapes, and a big squishy
peach.

Tom was just getting
started on a pineapple
when Mum snatched
it away.

'I've had enough of your nonsense,' she said crossly. 'You're not a gorilla. You're a boy.'

Tom showed her what he thought of boys. He lay on his back and waggled both feet in the air.

That made Mum extra mad. 'There'll be no more gorilla games in this house. Understand?' She pointed towards the stairs. 'It's early to bed for you, my boy!'

Tom did as he was told. Well . . . kind of. He rolled

head-over-heels across the
room. He hopped onto
the banisters and stood
balanced on one foot. He
wobbled up the handrail
instead of the stairs.

Mum didn't look pleased.
Nor did Dad.

Chapter Three

Next morning Mum couldn't
find Tom anywhere.

She searched his bed.
She crouched down and
peered *under* the bed.
She checked his cupboard.

'Where can he have got
to?' she wondered.

She found him at last
in the toybox. Fast asleep
amongst the board games
and Lego. And still in his
gorilla suit!

'How many times must
I tell you?' she said. 'These
silly gorilla games have got
to stop.' She handed him
his school uniform. 'Now get
yourself ready for school.'

Tom stared at his
uniform. He stared down

at his furry suit. Then he
put the uniform on over
the top.

When he went
downstairs, Mum said,
'Everyone will laugh
at you like that.'

Tom showed her he could laugh too. 'Hoo-hoo-hoo,' he said.

Mum sighed. 'Have it your own way,' she said.

And she took him off to school, gorilla suit and all.

Chapter Four

Tom arrived at school late.

The teacher gave him
a puzzled look. 'Who's this?
A new boy?'

'Waugh!' Tom said.

'Did you say Wal?' the
teacher asked. 'I suppose
that's short for Walter.'

'Waugh!' Tom repeated.
'Well, young Wal,' the
teacher said. 'Let's see how
good you are at sums.'

He held up a stick of chalk. 'If I add another piece of chalk to this one, how many will I have?'

Tom took the chalk and
broke it in two.

'Clever boy,' the teacher
said. 'Two is the right answer.

But what if I take two *away* from two? What then?'

Tom put both pieces of chalk in his mouth, chewed them up, and swallowed them.

The teacher beamed. 'Right again. Two from two leaves nothing.'

Tom soon showed he was just as good at language.

'What's the opposite of

peace?' the teacher asked
the class.

'Waugh!' Tom said.

'War it is. And who can
tell me what noise owls
make?'

'Hoo-hoo!' Tom laughed.

The teacher patted Tom's
furry head. 'I can see you're
a very bright lad,' he said.

Tom was even better
at games. Out in the
playground, he turned

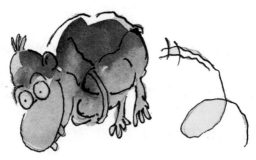

somersaults in mid-air.

He walked on his hands.

And he balanced a

football on his nose.

'I think we should make you class captain,' the teacher said.

All the kids agreed.

Chapter Five

There was a message for
Mum when she arrived
at the school. The principal
wanted to see her.

'What's Tom been up to
now?' she thought gloomily.

She found him sitting in
the principal's study,
as furry as ever.

'You must be very proud
of young Wal here,' the
principal said.

'That's not Wal,' Mum
said. 'That's my boy Tom.'
The principal frowned.
'You're surely mistaken,
Madam. His name is
Walter. He told us so.'

'Waugh!' Tom said.

'There you are. Wal for short. What's more, he's brilliant.'

'That's news to me,' Mum
said.

'No, he really is,' the
principal insisted. 'I'll prove
it to you.'

He turned to Tom.

'Here's a small test, young
Wal. Are you ready? What
does topsy-turvy mean?'

Tom gave a bored kind of
yawn and stood on his head.

'Exactly right,' the principal said. 'It means upside-down.'

He turned back to Tom's mum. 'You see. It's just as I said. He's quite the cleverest boy in the school.'

Round about then, Tom
gave another yawn. There
was a bunch of flowers
on the desk. He picked
them up and began
to munch the stems.

'Behave yourself,
Tom!' Mum said.

Tom didn't take the least
bit of notice. He had
finished the flowers. Now
he started chewing the
rubbery ends off the pencils.

He washed these
down with the principal's
ink. Then he leapt for the
light cord.

Swinging to and fro,
he dribbled ink onto the
principal's head.

Mum was deeply shocked.
So was the principal.

'I'm sorry about this,' Mum said. 'It's that silly gorilla suit. It always makes him act up.'

The principal dodged a drop of bright blue ink. 'Gorilla suit?' he said in a puzzled voice. 'I don't understand.'

Mum grabbed Tom and dragged him down.

'Here, I'll show you,' she said. 'It's one of these zip-on things. We bought it for his birthday.'

Holding Tom by one arm,
she felt along his back for
the zipper.

Except she couldn't find
one! There was no sign of

a zipper anywhere! All she
could feel was gorilla fur.
And underneath that,
gorilla muscles.

She turned him over and
stared hard at his face.
At his close-set eyes.
At his flattened nose.
At his very sharp teeth.

At his pointy head with its
tuft of fur.

'Good grief!' she cried.
'No wonder he ate his
pumpkin.'

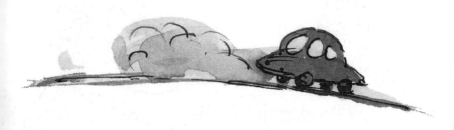

Chapter Six

Mum and Dad drove to the
zoo just before it closed.
They handed the baby
gorilla back to the keeper.

'You gave us this one
by mistake,' Dad told him.
'Our Tom's still in there.'

Mum dabbed at her eyes

with a tissue. 'You should
have taken more care,'
she sobbed. 'I expect he's
been eaten alive by now.'

'You can't please anybody these days,' the keeper grumbled.

He collected his net and took them along to the gorilla pen.

Sure enough, there was
Tom amongst the gorillas.
Mum spotted his zipper
when he swung on a tree.
He seemed perfectly happy.
In fact he did his best
to stay there in
the pen.

It took the keeper quite a while to catch him.

The keeper tipped Tom out of the net, right into Mum's arms. And the first thing she did was give him a cuddle.

'You're safe now, love,'
she sighed.

Then she tugged at the
zipper, and out popped Tom's
head. 'See!' she said happily.
'You're not a gorilla any more.

You're a boy again.'

'What do you say to that?'
Dad said with a laugh.

Tom looked at his mum
and dad. He looked back
at the gorillas in the pen.

'Waugh!' he grunted.

From Victor Kelleher

One day when I was being grumpy, my
wife said, 'You're acting like an animal.'
I said, 'What kind of animal?' And she
said, 'Oh . . . a gorilla or something.'

Well, that's how the story began . . .

No, not really. Just joking.

The truth is, I love gorillas and
wouldn't mind being one. How about you?

From Stephen Michael King

Now I've finished illustrating this book,
I think it's time for a change. Tomorrow
I'll go and buy myself a gorilla suit. I'll
wear it everywhere, while I'm working,
at the shops and even when I visit a school
for an author/illustrator visit. If anyone
tries to speak to me I'll just say 'Waugh!'

*Look out for these other
Happy Cat First Readers.*

No one believes in unicorns any more. Except Princess Lily, that is.
So when the king falls ill and the only thing that can cure him is
the magic of a unicorn, it's up to her to find one.
But can Lily find a magical unicorn in time?

THE LITTLEST PIRATE

SHERRYL CLARK

Nicholas Nosh is the littlest pirate in the world. He's not allowed to go to sea. 'You're too small,' said his dad. But when the fierce pirate Captain Red Beard kidnaps his family, Nicholas sets sail to rescue them!

Nobody is better at being bad than Buster Reed – he flicks
paint, says rude words to girls, sticks chewing gum under
the seats and wears the same socks for weeks at a time.
Naturally no one wants to know him. But Buster has a
secret – he would like a friend to play with.
How will he ever manage to find one?

When Anna Slept Over

Jane Godwin

Josie is Anna's best friend. Anna has played at Josie's house,
she's even stayed for dinner, but she has never slept over.
Until now…

The Magic Wand

Ursula Dubosarsky

Becky was cross with her little brother. 'If you don't leave me alone,' she said to him, 'I'll put a spell on you!' But she didn't mean to make him disappear!

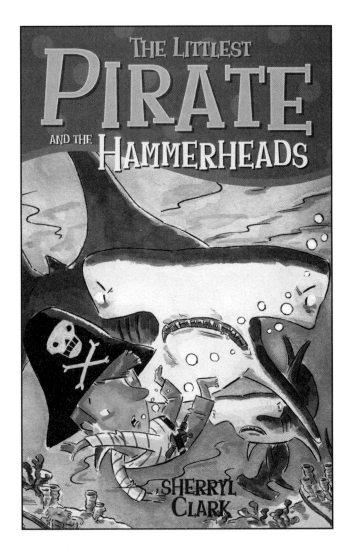

Nicholas Nosh, the littlest pirate in the world, has to rescue
his family's treasure which has been stolen by Captain
Hammerhead. But how can he outwit the sharks that are
guarding Captain Hammerhead's ship?

THE MERMAID'S TAIL

RAEWYN CAISLEY

Crystal longs to be a mermaid.
Her mother makes her a flashing silver tail. But it isn't like
being a proper mermaid. Then one night Crystal wears her
tail to bed...

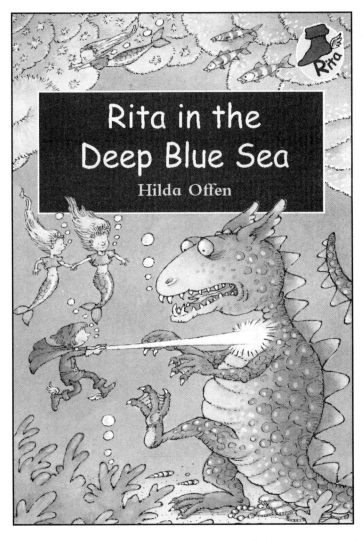

Rita's mother won't let her go on a boat with her brothers and sister. However, when she has changed into her Rescuer outfit she can ride on a turtle, tie an octopus in knots and even get the better of a mermaid-eating sea-monster!

Septimouse is the seventh son of a seventh son which makes him a
truly magical mouse. Septimouse can talk to cats and humans too
– he can even make them as tiny as he is. But the one thing he
can't seem to do is to get his paws on some cheese!

Septimouse needs all his magical powers when little Katie's
dad loses his job. But making humans mouse-sized, setting up a
magnificent cheese factory –it's all in a day's work for Septimouse!

Ann Jungman

SEPTIMOUSE
and the
CHEESE PARTY!

The supermouse has won the Cheese of the Year competition and
now longs for fame and fortune. If only his prize-winning cheese
recipe didn't have to be kept secret! Then disaster strikes –
only Septimouse can save the day!